D0065706

The Mystery of the Sand Castle

THREE COUSINS DETECTIVE CLUB®

9712

The Mystery of the Sand Castle

Elspeth Campbell Murphy
Illustrated by Joe Nordstrom

BETHANY HOUSE PUBLISHERS
MINNEAPOLIS, MINNESOTA 55438

Published by Bethany House Publishers
A Ministry of Bethany Fellowship International
11300 Hampshire Avenue South
Minneapolis, Minnesota 55438

Printed in the United States of America by
Bethany Press International, Minneapolis, Minnesota 55438

Library of Congress Cataloging-in-Publication Data
Murphy, Elspeth Campbell.
    The mystery of the sand castle / by Elspeth Campbell Murphy.
        p. cm. — (Three Cousins Detective Club ; 20)
    Summary: While visiting the resort town where their grandparents
live, Timothy and his cousins Titus and Sarah-Jane try to find out
what happened to a valuable locket "lost" on the beach.
    ISBN 1-55661-858-1
    [1. Cousins—Fiction. 2. Seashore—Fiction. 3. Mystery and
detective stories.] I. Title. II. Series: Murphy, Elspeth
Campbell. Three Cousins Detective Club ; 20.
PZ7.M95316Myfe   1998
[Fic]—dc21   97–53761
                                              CIP
                                                AC

ELSPETH CAMPBELL MURPHY has been a familiar name in Christian publishing for over fifteen years, with more than seventy-five books to her credit and sales reaching five million worldwide. She is the author of the best-selling series *David and I Talk to God* and *The Kids From Apple Street Church*, as well as the 1990 Gold Medallion winner *Do You See Me, God?* A graduate of Trinity College and Moody Bible Institute, Elspeth and her husband, Mike, make their home in Chicago, where she writes full time.

Contents

"There is a time for everything, and a season for every activity under heaven . . . a time to tear down and a time to build."

Ecclesiastes 3:1, 3b

1

Summer's End

"*Now* what do you want to do?" Timothy Dawson asked his cousins Sarah-Jane Cooper and Titus McKay.

"I don't know," replied Titus. "What do *you* want to do?"

"I asked you first," said Timothy.

Sarah-Jane just shrugged.

Usually the cousins had no trouble at all thinking up things to do. Their favorite thing to do was to solve mysteries. They even had a detective club.

But here they were at the beach, with sand and water and people as far as the eye could see. Only—no mysteries in sight.

Well, actually, there *had* been a little bit of a mystery. But the cousins hadn't been able to solve it, and that always made them cranky.

All in all, it was a good news/bad news kind of day.

The good news was that they were visiting the little resort town where their grandparents lived. They had gone swimming, of course. They had gone swimming until they looked like shivering prunes. That was the good news.

The bad news was that this was the last time they would be there before school started. Summer had somehow slipped away, and the cousins were not too happy about that.

Then there was the matter of the mystery.

2
A Little Mystery

*A*s mysteries go, it hadn't been that complicated.

A friend of their grandparents, Mrs. Hansen, had gone for a walk on the beach and lost her necklace.

What made it especially bad was that the necklace had been Mrs. Hansen's grandmother's. It looked like a locket on a chain. But when you opened the locket, inside was a beautiful little watch.

The cousins had seen the locket-watch before. So they knew exactly what to look for. It was a valuable antique. But even more important was its sentimental value.

"I would never have worn it for a day at the beach," Mrs. Hansen had explained. "But I was just going out for a little walk with my visitors after lunch. Then we met some other people from town, and we got to talking. I never noticed my watch was gone until later. The clasp must have been loose, but I never felt the necklace fall. And none of my friends saw it, either."

Naturally, Mrs. Hansen and her friends had retraced their steps. But the watch was nowhere to be found.

The cousins had desperately wanted to find the watch.

For a couple of reasons. Well, maybe three.

First of all, of course, they hated to see Mrs. Hansen so upset.

The second reason was that they wanted to believe the watch had simply been lost. Not stolen.

There had been a rash of burglaries and pickpocketings lately. This was bad news anywhere. But in a tourist town, it was *really* bad news. If crime was a problem, tourists wouldn't want to come to the town. And if tourists didn't come, motels and restaurants and shops would have to close.

There was a lot of pressure on the town

council to *do* something about it. Now. Their grandmother served on the town council, so the cousins had the inside scoop on some things. They knew she was puzzled and worried about the way things were disappearing around town.

And that was the third reason they wanted so much to find the watch.

Their grandmother was always bragging about how well behaved and smart they were. About what good detectives they were. And maybe the cousins wanted to show off a little bit by finding Mrs. Hansen's locket-watch. But mostly it was that they wanted to make their grandparents proud of them. Even though their grandparents always said they couldn't *be* any prouder. . . .

Timothy had even come up with the wonderful idea of asking a man with a metal detector to search the beach with them. But that had turned up nothing.

Mrs. Hansen had gone off to the tourist center, where there was a lost and found. But no one had turned in the watch. So Mrs. Hansen had gone sadly home.

It was no wonder, then, that the three cousins were feeling a little out of sorts.

They needed something new to do.

And that's when Titus came up with the idea of building a sand castle.

3

Castles

*T*itus knew a lot about castles. His father taught the history of the Middle Ages. That was the time—around a thousand years ago—when people were building castles.

The problem was, Sarah-Jane had read a lot of princess stories. She had very definite—and very different—ideas of what a castle should look like.

Titus picked up a stick and drew a diagram in the sand. He drew a square with circles at the corners. Inside the big square he drew a small square.

"OK," he said. "The big square is the wall with lookout towers at the four corners. The square in the middle is the main tower that the wall is protecting."

"Honestly, Ti!" wailed Sarah-Jane. "That castle just looks like a dumb old fort!"

"A castle *was* a dumb old fort!" replied Titus. He stopped, took a deep breath, and began again. "I *mean,* that's exactly what a castle was—a kind of fort. Rulers built castles to protect themselves and their people and their treasure from enemies.

"Over the years, castles got bigger and more complicated than this one. You could have inner walls and outer walls. You could have a moat and a drawbridge. But they were still basically *forts.* I just thought we should start with the simplest kind of castle, that's all."

Timothy loved the idea of a fort.

But Sarah-Jane wasn't buying it.

So Titus tried again.

He pointed to the big square and said, "Around the inside top of the wall, there was a walkway for the soldiers. It was called a *parapet.*"

He pointed to the open area inside the walls. "This courtyard around the tower was called the *bailey.*"

Timothy caught on right away to what

Titus was doing. Both boys knew how much Sarah-Jane liked interesting words.

Finally, Titus pointed to the square in the middle of the diagram and said—very, very casually—"The tower was called the *keep*."

Sarah-Jane narrowed her eyes and looked at Titus shrewdly. Timothy had no doubt that she had caught on, too.

"Oh, all right," she said. "We'll do it your way. We'll build a dumb old fort. But we'll use all those cool words to talk about it."

Timothy heaved a sigh of relief. He loved art and building things. His fingers were positively itching to dig in the cool, wet sand.

But they would need something other than fingers to build with. So they went off to find their grandparents and tell them about their plans for the castle.

4

The Bottomless Pit

*T*heir grandparents were right where they had left them, under the big beach umbrella. Their grandfather was dozing. Their grandmother was reading a magazine.

The cousins expected—when they had explained about the sand castle—that their grandmother would take them back to the house to scrounge for some sort of tools.

Instead, she just opened her tote bag.

Their grandmother's giant tote bag was kind of a family joke. Everyone called it "The Bottomless Pit."

It truly seemed to have no end, and the most amazing things came out of it. No one ever touched the bag except their grandmother. And yet it seemed to have something for everyone.

If you were hungry, out would come graham crackers, raisins, and bananas.

If you were cold, out would come sweat shirts, one-size-fits-all.

The cousins knew all about their grandmother's tote bag. Still, they were flabbergasted when she calmly reached in and pulled out sand pails and shovels. Not to mention some old spoons and a couple of spatulas.

Timothy, Titus, and Sarah-Jane stared at

one another. Silently they asked the question they had asked themselves so many times before:

How did she KNOW???

Their grandfather opened one eye and laughed up at them. He said, "Don't even try to figure it out. Just be glad that life with your grandmother is full of surprises."

This sounded like good advice, so the cousins just thanked their grandparents and went off to build a castle.

They hadn't gotten very far along on the castle when a chipper voice behind them said, "Why, hello there, munchkins! Spending a day at the beach, are we?"

5

Munchkins—Not!

*T*imothy and his cousins glanced at one another and inwardly groaned. They couldn't groan out loud because their grandparents were very big on basic politeness—even to people who got on your nerves.

And there was no getting around it, thought Timothy. Mr. Dockery got on their nerves. It was hard to say why exactly. He was a very distinguished-looking gentleman who served on the town council with their grandmother.

Mr. Dockery was always cheerful and charming. He always made a fuss over the cousins. But, thought Timothy, it was as if he was making a fuss over you without actually noticing you.

For example, he didn't seem to realize how old they were. Timothy didn't know about little kids—but when you were ten years old and going into fifth grade, *and* you had solved a few mysteries, you definitely did *NOT* want to be called *munchkin*.

Plus, Mr. Dockery was forever pulling quarters out of their ears.

It was just a trick, of course. It was supposed to be charming and funny, but somehow it was just annoying. Maybe it was because they never got to keep the quarters. The money always disappeared back into Mr. Dockery's pockets.

Still, their grandparents expected good behavior.

So when Mr. Dockery exclaimed, "And what is *this,* munchkins? Building a sand castle, are we?" the cousins knew better than to say, "Well, duh!"

Instead, they just nodded politely. They might not have been able to prove today what great detectives they were. But at least they could prove they had nice manners.

Timothy glanced over at his grandparents. He could have sworn he saw the corners of his

grandmother's mouth twitch. And his grandfather wink at him.

Maybe, thought Timothy, Mr. Dockery
got on the grown-ups' nerves, too.

"My dear Grace!" Mr. Dockery said to their grandmother. "What's this I hear about Mrs. Hansen losing—a locket, was it? I was talking to her and her friends on the beach earlier today. I'm afraid I never noticed if she was wearing any jewelry, so *I* don't know when she could have lost it. I don't suppose it's turned up?"

Mrs. Gordon shook her head sadly. "No, and I don't think Annabelle is very hopeful about getting it back."

"Well, I hate to say this," said Mr. Dockery grimly. "But I'm wondering: Did she lose it? Or was it stolen? It's these dreadful pickpockets! The town council must get to the bottom of this, Grace. We really must."

Before their grandmother could answer, another friend of theirs came up to chat. This lady was on the council, too. For a few minutes they talked about the mysterious thefts. But then the conversation got pretty boring.

The cousins were only half listening anyway. They were much more interested in their sand castle.

6

A Time to Build

*I*t had been Titus's idea to build the castle. But Timothy knew more about building things. So Sarah-Jane and Titus followed Timothy's lead.

The cousins had a rule that said it was OK for one cousin to sort of be the boss of something. AS LONG AS THAT COUSIN DIDN'T GET BOSSY.

Timothy didn't get bossy, so the work on their sand castle went along well.

They picked their spot carefully.

It had to be close enough to the shore so that they could get plenty of good wet sand. Water is what holds the sand together for building.

But the castle had to be far enough back from the shore so that waves wouldn't wreck it.

Once they had the spot picked out, they

had to get the ground all flat and smooth. This was so the castle would stand up straight and not fall over. Their plan was to build the middle tower—the keep—first. Then they would build the outer walls around it to protect it. While they worked, they tuned in and out to what the grown-ups were saying.

They heard the new lady say to Mr. Dockery, "Edward, I love that jacket you're wearing. My husband's birthday is coming up, and he's so hard to buy for! But I really think he would love a jacket like that one. Do you mind if I take a look at it?"

Mr. Dockery seemed to hesitate for just a fraction of a second. Timothy thought that maybe he didn't like the idea of someone else having a jacket like his. Timothy noticed people a lot. He knew that some people liked to look like everybody else. And some people liked to look different.

But Mr. Dockery exclaimed, "My dear lady! I'm so glad you like it. And how kind of you to say so! By all means, take a closer look. And while you're doing that, I will help my little friends with their sand castle."

7

The T.C.D.C.

*T*imothy looked at his cousins in sheer panic. They were looking back at him, horror-stricken, as if to say, "*You're* in charge here. *Do something!*"

But what could he do? Throw himself on the sand, screaming, "Over my dead body!"?

Not exactly.

"Ah, I see you're building a keep," said Mr. Dockery. "That is what you call the central tower of a castle. I have visited some castles, so I know a little bit about them, you see. Do you mind?"

Without waiting for an answer, Mr. Dockery set to work on the keep.

Timothy sat back and watched with a strange mixture of feelings.

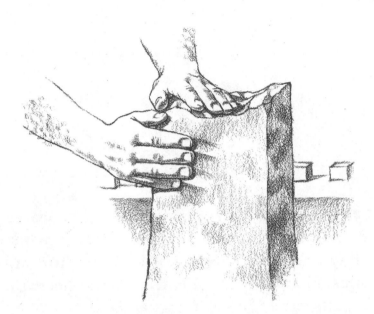

On the one hand, it was really irritating to have someone messing with their castle. But on the other hand, Mr. Dockery was doing a really *great* job. His hands seemed to fly—shaping and patting and smoothing the keep. That done, he grabbed the spatula and began carving notches around the top.

"Now, children, these are called—"

"Crenels," said Titus.

"Why, my dear boy! You are exactly right!" exclaimed Mr. Dockery. "However did you know that?" He sounded astonished that three such adorable little munchkins could know anything at all.

"We know a lot of things," said Sarah-Jane in a tight voice.

Timothy could tell she was trying to keep from blowing up. "We're the T.C.D.C.," he said quickly, in order to help her out.

"Indeed!" cried Mr. Dockery. "How absolutely delightful!"

He stopped. It suddenly seemed to occur to him that he had no idea what Timothy was talking about. "What's a 'teesy-deesy'?" he asked.

"It's letters," explained Sarah-Jane, sounding a lot calmer now. "Capital T. Capital C. Capital D. Capital C. It stands for the Three Cousins Detective Club."

"Detectives!" exclaimed Mr. Dockery. "What fun! And have you solved any mysteries, munchkins?"

"One or two," said Titus with a perfectly straight face.

"How nice!" said Mr. Dockery. "And did you help Mrs. Hansen look for her watch?"

"Yes," said Timothy. And he couldn't help adding, "Of *course* we did! We did a very thorough job. We looked everywhere."

Mr. Dockery shook his head sadly. "But you didn't find it. Ah, well. You mustn't blame yourselves. I'm quite sure the locket will never be found."

With that, Mr. Dockery rose and clapped the sand from his hands. He seemed to have lost interest in the sand castle.

Which was a tremendous relief to the three cousins.

Mr. Dockery reached for his jacket and said to them, "Well, I really must be going. This has been great fun. Good-bye, my little Sherlocks. Take care!"

The cousins stared after him. Then they looked at one another again, all thinking the same thing:

"My little Sherlocks"??? Oh, puh-leeze!

8

The "Itch"

Something was bothering Timothy. But he couldn't figure out what.

It didn't seem as if *anything* should be bothering him. After all, Mr. Dockery wasn't hanging around anymore, trying to help. But in a strange sort of way, he *was* helping them. Because—when it came time to build the outer walls and the corner towers, the cousins were able to copy the work Mr. Dockery had done on the keep.

And the results—if they did say so themselves—were spectacular. The castle was coming along beautifully.

But something was bothering Timothy. What?

There was something he needed to ask his

grandparents. But he didn't know what it was.

The feeling was frustrating, to say the least.

It was like when you had an itch. But when you tried to scratch the itch, you couldn't even *find* it. So there you were, scratching all over the place without hitting the itchy spot.

That's what this felt like. Except—this was an "itchy question" in Timothy's mind. He knew if he could get an answer to that question, it would be like scratching an itch. The problem was, he couldn't even *find* the question in his head.

Wait a minute. . . . It had something to do with something someone had said . . . something that didn't make sense. . . . Not unless . . .

But no. As soon as he thought he had grabbed the question, it was gone.

It was *extremely* frustrating, to say the least.

Timothy knew that sometimes the best way to remember something is to forget about it. But that is easier said than done. It isn't easy to stop your thoughts from running in circles. Sometimes the only thing to do is think about something else.

So Timothy turned all of his attention to

the sand castle. He got into a kind of soothing rhythm—shaping, patting, smoothing. Just as Mr. Dockery had done on the keep.

On and on Timothy worked.

He forgot all about his question.

Until it popped up—full-blown—in his head.

9

Questions

When Timothy told his cousins what he was thinking, their mouths dropped open in surprise. But they didn't try to argue with him. And they didn't call him crazy.

"It's a good question, all right," said Titus.

"It certainly is," said Sarah-Jane. "Because—how in the world did he know?"

Sarah-Jane and Titus went along when Timothy went to ask his question. But, of course, since it was Timothy's question, he got to do the talking.

"Grandma," said Timothy. "When you and Mr. Dockery and Grandpa and that other lady were talking about Mrs. Hansen's locket . . . did you tell Mr. Dockery what it looked like? I mean, did you tell him what it *was*?"

One of the *many* things the cousins loved about their grandparents was that they didn't ask you a million questions before they answered one of yours.

Instead, their grandparents were quiet for a minute, thinking back.

At last their grandmother said, "Mr. Dockery had heard that Mrs. Hansen lost a locket. But he said he never noticed her jewelry when he was talking to her. And none of us mentioned the details of what it looked like."

"Positive?" asked Timothy

"Positive," said his grandmother.

"Tim!" said Sarah-Jane, unable to keep quiet any longer. "You were right!"

"Yes!" agreed Titus. "It's just what you thought."

Now that the grandparents had let Timothy get his question out, they had a question of their own.

"Timothy," said their grandfather. "What's going on?"

Timothy took a deep breath and tried to explain calmly. (It didn't exactly help that Titus and Sarah-Jane were bouncing up and down.)

"OK," said Timothy. "When Mr. Dockery was helping us to build the keep, we told him about the T.C.D.C. And he said, 'How nice. Did you help Mrs. Hansen look for her watch?' That's what he called it—a watch. Right, guys?"

Sarah-Jane and Titus nodded so hard it looked like their heads might pop off and go rolling across the sand like beach balls.

Timothy continued. From the way his grandparents were looking at him, he could tell they knew what he was going to ask next. But he said it anyway. "And that's my question: If Mr. Dockery never saw the locket, and no one told him what it looked like, then how did he know it had a watch inside?"

10

A Weird Little Lie

*F*or a long time nobody spoke. At last their grandfather said, "Timothy, where are we going with all this?"

Timothy shrugged and said, "I don't know exactly. It just seems like a weird little thing to lie about. I mean, why do people lie? To cover up something they think might get them in trouble. Right? So why would you lie about knowing what a missing necklace looks like? Unless—!"

"Unless you're the one who took it," said Sarah-Jane simply.

Again, they were all quiet, thinking about this.

"But *when*?" asked their grandmother.

"Mrs. Hansen was wearing the locket on the beach today."

"And Mr. Dockery talked to her on the beach today," said Timothy. "It would be too risky for him to lie and say he wasn't there."

"But that's just it, isn't it?" asked their grandmother. "There were a lot of people around. We know Mr. Dockery didn't snatch the locket and run with it. Could he really have gotten hold of it without anyone noticing? How?"

Titus shrugged and said, "Hey, what can I tell you? All I know is that the guy can pull quarters out of our ears."

11

A Locket in the Pocket?

*T*imothy saw his grandparents look at each other in alarm. He could tell what they were thinking. *Mr. Dockery?! A pickpocket?!*

"Could anyone really do that?" said their grandmother. "Take the necklace without the wearer knowing it?"

"I imagine so," their grandfather replied. "There was a lot of distraction. People were standing around talking. He could have pretended to brush away a bug, something like that. It would take no time at all to get the locket and slip it into his pocket."

"Except it wasn't in his pocket," said Timothy.

Everyone turned to him in surprise.

"What?" said Titus. "How do you know that?"

"I don't," said Timothy. "Not for sure, anyway. But think back to what Mr. Dockery was wearing. He had on plain bathing trunks and a plain T-shirt. No pockets there."

"He was wearing that jacket as a kind of beach cover-up," said Sarah-Jane. "It had pockets."

"Exactly," said Timothy. "But that lady asked to look at it. And Mr. Dockery *let* her. If there had been a locket in the pocket, wouldn't she have noticed? Would Mr. Dockery have wanted to take that risk? I don't think so. That's why I said the locket wasn't in the pocket."

"Then where was it?" asked Sarah-Jane. "Do you think he had already hidden it somewhere else?"

They all automatically glanced up and down the beach.

"Not a whole lot of good hiding places," said Titus. "You could bury something in the sand, I suppose. But how would you remember exactly where you put it? And how could you be sure someone else wouldn't come along and dig it up before you could get back to it?"

"Maybe that's what happened," said Sarah-Jane. "Maybe somebody else found the locket and kept it. Because *we* sure didn't find it!"

"Neither did the guy with the metal detector," said Titus.

Their grandfather said, "It seems to me we're getting ahead of ourselves here. We're suspecting Mr. Dockery of a serious crime. And I don't mean getting on people's nerves. That's irritating, but it's not illegal!"

Their grandmother added, "Mr. Dockery is the one on the council who's most upset about the pickpocketings. Are we saying he's doing that as a cover? That *he's* the pickpocket himself? If we had found the necklace in his pocket, that would be one thing. But I think Timothy's right. I don't see how the locket *could* have been in the jacket. And if it wasn't in the pocket, what did he do with it? We must be careful not to jump to conclusions."

Sarah-Jane and Titus nodded seriously.

But Timothy looked up and said quietly, "I know what Mr. Dockery did with the necklace. At least—I have a pretty good idea."

12

Almost Positive

Being almost positive was not the same thing at all as being positive.

When you were positive about something, you could relax. You knew you were right. No problem.

But being *almost* positive was *awful*. You *didn't* know for sure that you were right. And you *couldn't* relax because you were dying of curiosity. You just *had* to find out.

But sometimes finding out wasn't just up to you. You had to talk other people into it.

And that wasn't always easy.

As Timothy discovered when he told his cousins what he wanted to do.

"WHAT?!" cried Titus. "After all that work? No way!"

"And what if you're wrong?" said Sarah-Jane. "Do you really want to wreck something for nothing?"

"I'm not talking about wrecking the whole thing," said Timothy. "Just that one part of it."

Titus and Sarah-Jane were quiet.

Timothy knew they were fascinated by his idea. But he also knew that they had big doubts about it. Well, so did he.

But if there was even a chance they could get Mrs. Hansen's locket back, didn't they at least have to try?

He said as much to his cousins. And that was enough to swing them over to his side.

Timothy glanced at his grandparents. They had wanted the cousins to work this out for themselves. But Timothy could tell they thought the cousins were doing the right thing. That helped.

"I just wish we had X-ray vision," muttered Titus. "So we could see through sand."

"No," said Sarah-Jane. "But we have the next best thing. We can *hear* through sand. Look!"

The man with the metal detector was not

far off. He had helped out once before. Maybe he would again.

The cousins went to talk to him.

"I'm sorry to bother you," said Timothy. "But we're missing something. And we think it might have gotten dropped into our sand castle. Only—we don't want to wreck it for nothing. So could you—?"

"Sure thing," said the man.

He came back with them and ran the metal detector over the keep as Timothy asked him to.

"Yep," the man said. "There's something in there all right. No telling what it is, though."

"That's OK," said Timothy. "We'll soon find out."

13

A Time to Tear Down

*T*he man with the metal detector went his way, looking for coins and other interesting things.

The cousins and their grandparents gathered around the sand castle.

Now that it was actually time to *do* it, Timothy wanted to run through the theory again.

"OK," he said. "I think Mr. Dockery is the pickpocket. I think he saw Mrs. Hansen's locket and saw that it was valuable. I think he saw a chance to steal it. So he did. And he slipped it into his pocket. When he was able to look at the locket up close, he saw that it was actually a watch.

"Everything was going fine for him—*until* that lady asked to see his jacket. What could he do? Mr. Dockery didn't want to say no, because he always pretends to be so charming. Also, he didn't want to do anything that looked the least bit suspicious. But he couldn't just turn over the jacket with the locket in it.

"So what does he do? He hesitates for a split second. Then he sees the *perfect* hiding place. So he slips the locket into his hand. Like a kind of magic trick. And then he slips the locket from his hand into the keep. Another trick.

"Remember how he was patting the sand? We never suspected a thing. And we're *detectives*!"

"*No* one suspected a thing," said their grandmother.

"Yes," said Titus. "It was the perfect cover. A nice man playing in the sand with the little munchkins."

Their grandparents laughed.

"I almost feel a little sorry for Mr. Dockery," said their grandfather. "The poor guy had no idea who he was dealing with."

"Well," said Timothy. "I think that's right—if I do say so myself. I think his plan was just to leave the locket where it was in the keep, figuring he could come back after we'd gone and get the locket. It would be risky, but what could he do? He was counting on us not wanting to wreck the castle, I think."

"We don't want to wreck the castle," said Sarah-Jane.

"But we have to," said Titus. "At least the keep."

Timothy took a deep breath. "Then let's do it," he said.

14

Treasure

"**W**ait a minute," said their grandfather. "No sense advertising what we're doing."

He made an elaborate show of looking up at the sky and moving the beach umbrella for better shade. What he was really doing, of course, was blocking the sand castle from view as much as possible.

The three cousins were super-careful about taking the keep apart.

For one thing, they didn't want to wreck the walls or any more of the keep than they absolutely had to.

For another thing, they didn't want it to look as if they were taking anything apart at all. They wanted it to look as if they were just adding some decorations or something. So they dug down carefully using their spoons and spatulas.

They didn't have to dig far.

"I've got something," Timothy whispered.

Titus and Sarah-Jane leaned forward as Timothy carefully pulled out a gold chain that glinted in the sun.

"So cool!" breathed Sarah-Jane.

"EX-cellent!" agreed Titus.

"Neat-O!" whispered Timothy.

Quickly he gathered the chain and the locket up in his hand. He wasn't as good at this sort of thing as Mr. Dockery. But, for someone who wasn't a pickpocket, Timothy did very well.

Still, he was glad to slip the locket-watch into his grandfather's capable hands. "Grandpa," he said. "We need to put this in a safe place until we can give it back to Mrs. Hansen."

His grandfather replied in his most super-serious voice. (Which meant he was joking.) He said, "My dear children. I know of a cavern so deep and dark, they say the sun never shines there. We will wrap this treasure in my handkerchief and drop it into . . ."

"The Bottomless Pit," said Timothy, Titus, and Sarah-Jane all together.

They were talking, of course, about their grandmother's tote bag.

15

A Time for Everything

"*B*ut what about Mr. Dockery?" asked Titus when the locket-watch was safely in the bag. "He's going to come back later and see we've been digging in the keep. He's going to put two and two together and realize that we're on to him. Then he'll clear out and get clean away."

"Oh, I don't think that will happen," said his grandmother, patting his shoulder.

"Why not, Grandma?" asked Titus.

"Because Mr. Dockery isn't the only one with a few tricks up his sleeve," she replied. "When Mr. Dockery comes back tonight, he's going to find the keep exactly as he left it. And he's going to reach in and pull out a chain. And a few people will be here to see him do it. Then the charming Mr. Dockery will have some heavy-duty explaining to do."

Her grandchildren stared at her open-mouthed.

When he could finally pick his chin up off the sand, Timothy said, "So—are you going to put the necklace back for him to find?"

"No," said his grandmother thoughtfully. "He might be able to hide it again. I don't want to risk that. We will need to use a substitute."

"But where in the world are we going to find a substitute for the locket?" asked Sarah-Jane.

By way of reply, her grandmother simply opened her bag.

Everyone laughed.

"Ask a silly question!" cried Sarah-Jane.

Out came a shiny metal chain with a trim little whistle on the end.

The cousins laughed even harder when they saw what it was. They had come running whenever they heard that whistle for as long as they could remember.

"Mr. Dockery will love this, don't you think?" their grandmother asked them. "It's used for calling munchkins, and we all know how much he likes them. Now, be good little munchkins and hide the whistle in the tower. Grandpa will help you rebuild it. Grandma has a few calls to make."

When their grandmother got back from the pay phone, the cousins and their grandparents made a show of packing up for the day and going home.

Pretending to go home.

Actually, they were going to stick around for a while. The cousins were going to have supper at the hot dog stand and lie low at the top of a sand dune to watch what happened. The grown-ups didn't want kids getting too close. That was OK by the cousins. They knew that sometimes you just have to turn over the whole sting operation to your grandmother.

Before they left, the cousins took a long last look at their beautiful sand castle. Timothy gave a contented sigh. But it was a sigh tinged with sadness. "It's so beautiful," he said. "I wish it could last forever."

"Nothing lasts forever," said Titus wistfully. "Not even real castles. Most of them are in ruins now."

"There's a time for everything under the sun," said their grandfather.

"Good-bye, castle," said Sarah-Jane.
"Good-bye, parapets. Good-bye, crenels.
Good-bye, bailey. Good-bye, keep."

They were actually getting a little weepy
when their grandfather leaned over and said in
his super-serious voice, "Those hot dogs
aren't going to eat themselves, you know.

Come on. We have work to do."

———

Their grandmother's "sting" went off without a hitch. But she was giving the cousins all the credit. Bragging about her grandchildren was practically her life's work.

So, all in all, it had been a very good day indeed.

Later that night, when they were back at the house, Timothy turned to his cousins. He said, "*Now* what do you want to do?"

"I don't know," said Titus.

"What do *you* want to do?" asked Sarah-Jane.

"I asked you first," said Timothy.

The End

Series for Young Readers*
From Bethany House Publishers

★ ★ ★

THE ADVENTURES OF CALLIE ANN
by *Shannon Mason Leppard*

Readers will giggle their way through the true-to-life escapades of Callie Ann Davies and her many North Carolina friends.

★ ★ ★

BACKPACK MYSTERIES
by *Mary Carpenter Reid*

This excitement-filled mystery series follows the mishaps and adventures of Steff and Paulie Larson as they strive to help often-eccentric relatives crack their toughest cases.

★ ★ ★

THE CUL-DE-SAC KIDS
by *Beverly Lewis*

Each story in this lighthearted series features the hilarious antics and predicaments of nine endearing boys and girls who live on Blossom Hill Lane.

★ ★ ★

RUBY SLIPPERS SCHOOL
by *Stacy Towle Morgan*

Join the fun as home-schoolers Hope and Annie Brown visit fascinating countries and meet inspiring Christians from around the world!

★ ★ ★

THREE COUSINS DETECTIVE CLUB®
by *Elspeth Campbell Murphy*

Famous detective cousins Timothy, Titus, and Sarah-Jane learn compelling Scripture-based truths while finding—and solving—intriguing mysteries.

* (ages 7–10)

9611

4.1/40